Have a joyful day!

Bobette
Stanbridge

A Joyful Day was produced by

The Bobette Art Co. in 2008

It is a book from the Bobette's Bunkies series.

To order prints or this book, E-mail:
thebobetteartco@yahoo.com
or visit our web page at www.thebobetteartco.com

I would like to thank Michelle Zymowski at Printing Prep, Buffalo, NY for all her help, my children Brahman & Tiffany, and my grandchildren Emily & Ethan for their inspiration.

A Joyful Day

Written and Illustrated by
Bobette Stanbridge

Introducing a new type of picture book that
has been created to engage children in
conversations about important subjects that
are guides to successful lives.

Enjoy and Have Fun!

t was a warm, sunny day with a soft breeze that made it an easy glide for Chirpy bird.

She caught the wind and let it carry her up and down, down and up. She was having a great time, and occasionally she would land on a branch or a fence to chat with some of her friends.

hirpy bird had many friends. She had tree friends, flower friends, and rock friends. She had animal and insect friends and even some people friends.

On this particular day, she found herself flying around Miss Apra Cott tree. It was the middle of March and Apra's white blossoms were in full bloom. How beautiful she looked. Chirpy said, "Hello, Miss Apra." Apra bowed her head to say hello and spread her branches to welcome her.

"It looks like you are going to have a bounty of apricots this year. I must be sure to tell Miss Annie elephant and Julie so they can pick them." Just then she heard music coming through the meadow. Chirpy bird loved music, and she would sing any chance she got. Apra Cott tree liked to sway to music and always hoped for a breeze when the wondrous melodies were heard. The wind was just right, and the two friends began to dance and sing in harmony.

Chirpy decided to fly up high to see who was making such wonderful music. It was her friends Julie, Miss Annie elephant, Benjamin Bear, Smooch the pooch, & Meeka mouse. They had a band playing the flute, trumpet, drum, & tambourine. Chirpy got really excited and flew back to tell Apra she was going to go sing with the band and would be back later.

hirpy bird flew over to the band and began to fly around and sing and dance with the group. It was really fun, and all of the trees and flowers were really enjoying the wonderful music.

Smooch pooch was very talented and flexible and could actually play the drum and trumpet at the same time. Julie's flute playing seemed to be a call to the fairies. Sometimes Julie would sing with the group, and Chirpy loved to harmonize with her.

hen Julie had to go home for lunch, Miss Annie elephant and Smooch pooch walked her home. Then Smooch pooch remembered he forgot to water his flower friends and ran off. On the way to Julie's house, Miss Annie decided to grab a bite to eat and reached into a tree to pick some leaves as she passed by.

t was a Jacaranda tree with beautiful Purple flowers. Miss Annie accidentally picked some of Jackie Jacaranda's flowers and Jackie became startled and flung her branches at Miss Annie to stop her. Miss Annie lost her balance and tripped and fell. "Hey what did you do that for?" asked Annie. Jackie thought, "My flowers are not for eating. They are to make the world a more beautiful place."

Then she realized Miss Annie had fallen and felt sorry she had caused her to fall. Miss Annie looked in her hand and noticed she had some purple flowers. She knew she wasn't supposed to pick her flowers to eat and looked up at Jackie and apologized.

nnie was hurt, so she and Julie moved away from Jackie and found another tree to sit under. Julie put down a blanket for her to sit on and called in some of their friends to help take care of her. Tommy the Turtle helped to raise her leg, and Sir Gus Grasshopper brought some flowers to raise her spirits.

Sir Gus asked his Fairy friends to tell him what Miss Annie needed to help her heal and was told that Saw Palmetto was used to reduce swelling. So Sir Gus Grasshopper brought the Saw Palmetto essence and gave it to Julie to drop on Miss Annie's tongue. Julie then wrapped her wounded trunk and knee with a bandage, and they sat for a while until Miss Annie elephant felt a little better.

eanwhile, Smooch pooch arrived at his destination and was greeted by his flower friends. Each flower offers its beauty and essence to all who see & smell them. The flowers were dancing and having a great time as Smooch watered them. They were happy that they were being watered because it helped them grow. Smooch was sure he heard them singing "A Flower knows that Happiness grows."

Smooch the Pooch was taught by his grandmother that each flower has special qualities, such as the Cosmos flower's quality is clarity of speech, the Rhododendron helps to increase one's energy, and Impatiens is for patience. Begonias help one feel good and Baby Blue Eyes help one to feel supported.

 hirpy bird had gone to take a nap on a cloud that she called home, but instead of her nap she had a surprise visit by her friend Meeka Mouse.

Meeka found a helium balloon and decided to take a trip up to Chirpy's cloud home. They floated around all day and spoke of the great views from so high up. Chirpy was pleased that Meeka was brave enough to take this trip to see her because she was usually a scaredy mouse. But they were great friends and Meeka loved their time together. She just focused on how much she would enjoy visiting with Chirpy, and this helped her overcome her fear.

CHIRPY'S PLACE

hen it was time for Meeka mouse to go home, Chirpy bird flew down with her to make sure she had a safe journey. Meeka was married to Jake mouse, who had come from New York City. Jake was very brave and was always there to protect Meeka.

When they arrived, Jake was putting all of his tools in order. He liked things in their place because it made it easier to find them when he needed them. They sat down together and sipped some herbal tea in their garden. Their garden had mint, licorice, chamomile, and raspberry leaves growing that they used for their tea. It was very delicious.

hirpy said goodbye and flew away. As she flew she saw Miss Annie elephant resting under a tree. Julie, Sir Gus Grasshopper, and Tommy Turtle had gone their separate ways so Miss Annie elephant was alone. Chirpy thought she would join her for an afternoon nap since she had missed her nap earlier. She found a hole in the tree above her head and flew in.

 iss Annie elephant was always changing colors with her moods. and now she was a very pretty purple blue. She fell asleep and had a wonderful dream of herself, Chirpy bird, Selina butterfly and some of her flower friends dancing together. She was pink in her dream.

You Make Me

Bobette © 2005

So Very Happy

 elina butterfly was so happy that she displayed all of her colors and patterns for everyone to see. She looked amazing and beautiful as she expressed herself.

 iss Annie elephant continued to dream. She was now dreaming she was a performer in the circus and was doing a balancing act with her friends, Smooch, Selina, Benjamin, Chirpy and Jake.

At the end of her act she took a bow, and the whole audience was applauding her and shouting how beautiful she was. She had a pretty dress on for her finale, and when the circus was over, she went outside and felt the warmth of the sun and thought about how beautiful she felt and what a wonderful day she had. Soon she awoke and felt refreshed and happy. All was well and her fall seemed only like a distant memory. Her bandages had all disappeared.

hen Benjamin bear left the band, he went home to hibertate. First he was very hungry, so he ate a delicious fish dinner.

Hibertation is a way to quiet your mind from your thoughts. It is a great way to feel peaceful, and when you stop hibertating your thoughts are usually better, happier, and more productive.

hen Benjamin bear lit a nice fire in his fireplace and had some wonderful visions of taking a train ride down to the sea with his friends.

They heard some very beautiful music playing on an acoustic guitar. They had no idea where it came from, but it made their trip so much more enjoyable.

hen they got to the sea, there was a wooden raft, a blue-and-white checkered blanket and a picnic basket waiting for them for their fishing trip filled with yummy things to eat.

Jake and Annie loved to pretend to be pirates, Chirpy stood watch as their lookout and Benjamin did the fishing.

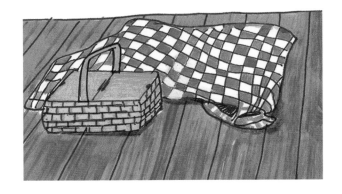

e saw that Smooch pooch and Julie had a good book they wanted to read so they took a blanket to lay on the ground and sat under an apple tree while Julie read out loud.

Benjamin bear awoke from his hibertation and decided that tomorrow would be a great day to take a train to the ocean for his fishing trip. Chirpy woke up and flew back to Apra Cott tree and told her of her day's adventures. Tommy turtle went home to Tallulah turtle and Sir Gus Grasshopper and Smooch pooch went home too.

he next day was joyful because all the visions Benjamin bear had in his hibertation came true.

When Julie arrived home she sat down to a nice dinner with her family. After dinner she helped clean up the dishes and counters and decided to paint a picture.

She thought about what a fun day she had and how happy she felt, so she painted a picture of some of her friends and added the word happy many times to her picture because that is how she felt. And so once again a wonderful time was had by all.